Originally published in French under the title *La tournée de facteur souris*
by Les Editions Casterman s.a.

© 2015 Casterman
Text and illustrations by Marianne Dubuc

English translation © 2015 Kids Can Press
English translation by Yvette Ghione

Kids Can Press acknowledges the financial support of the Government
of Ontario, through the Ontario Media Development Corporation's
Ontario Book Initiative.

Published in Canada by   Published in the U.S. by
Kids Can Press Ltd.   Kids Can Press Ltd.
25 Dockside Drive   2250 Military Road
Toronto, ON M5A 0B5   Tonawanda, NY 14150

www.kidscanpress.com

The text is set in Gill Sans.

English edition edited by Yvette Ghione

This book is smyth sewn casebound.
Manufactured in China in 4/2015 by South China Printing Co. Ltd.

CM 15 0 9 8 7 6 5 4 3 2 1

Library and Archives Canada Cataloguing in Publication

Dubuc, Marianne, 1980– [Tournée de facteur souris. English]
    Mr. Postmouse's rounds / Marianne Dubuc.

Translation of: La tournée de facteur souris.
English translation by Yvette Ghione.
ISBN 978-1-77138-572-5 (bound)

    I. Ghione, Yvette, translator II. Title. III. Title: Tournée de facteur
souris. English.

PS8607.U2245T6913 2015   jC843'.6   C2015-900439-X

Kids Can Press is a *Corus*™ Entertainment company

Mr. Postmouse's Rounds

MARIANNE DUBUC

Kids Can Press

It's Monday, and Mr. Postmouse is starting his rounds.
He carefully loads up his little wagon and sets off.

He makes his first delivery to Mr. Bear, who has been waiting for a letter from his aunt Ursula.

Next, Mr. Postmouse delivers a large parcel to the Rabbit family.

Phew! Nothing for Mr. Snake today,
he thinks with relief.

At the Birds', Mr. Postmouse
climbs up, up, up into the trees.
Luckily, he isn't afraid of heights.

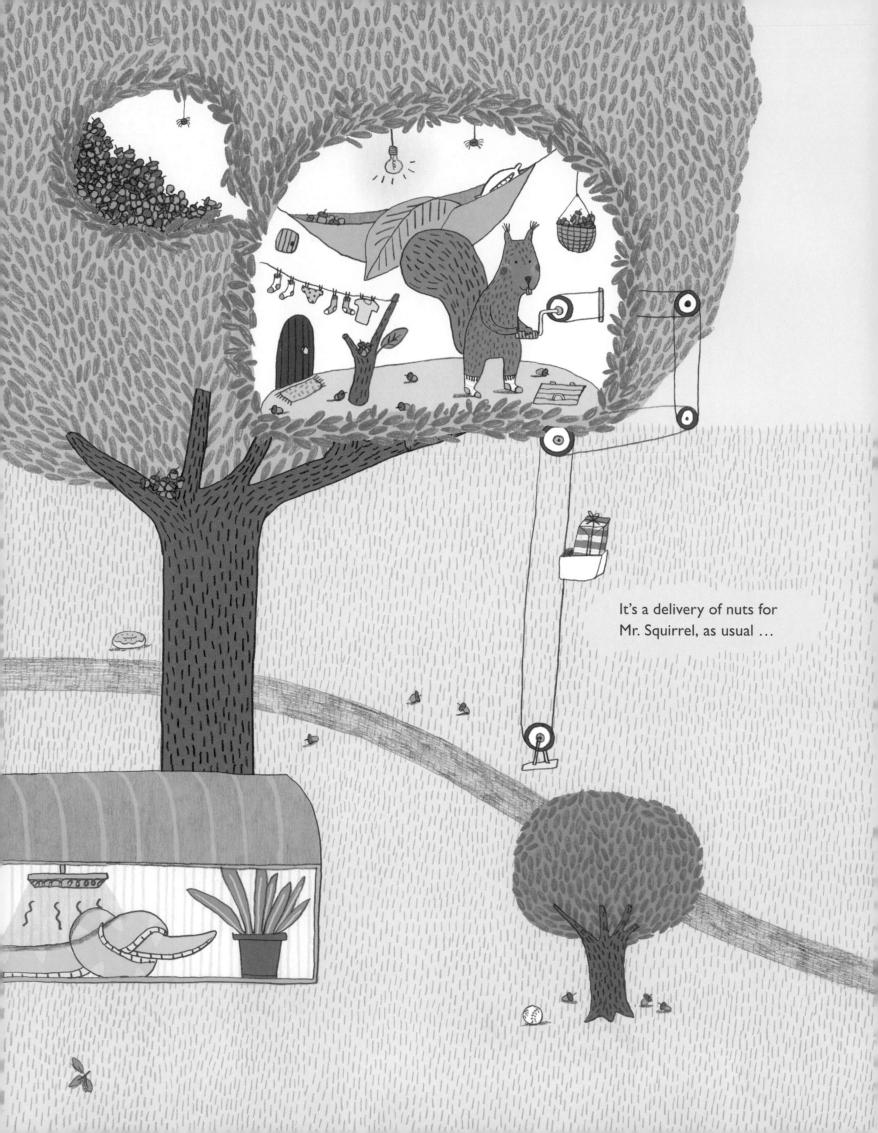

It's a delivery of nuts for
Mr. Squirrel, as usual ...

Then it's time for lunch. Mr. Postmouse stops at his friend Mr. Dragon's for some barbecue.

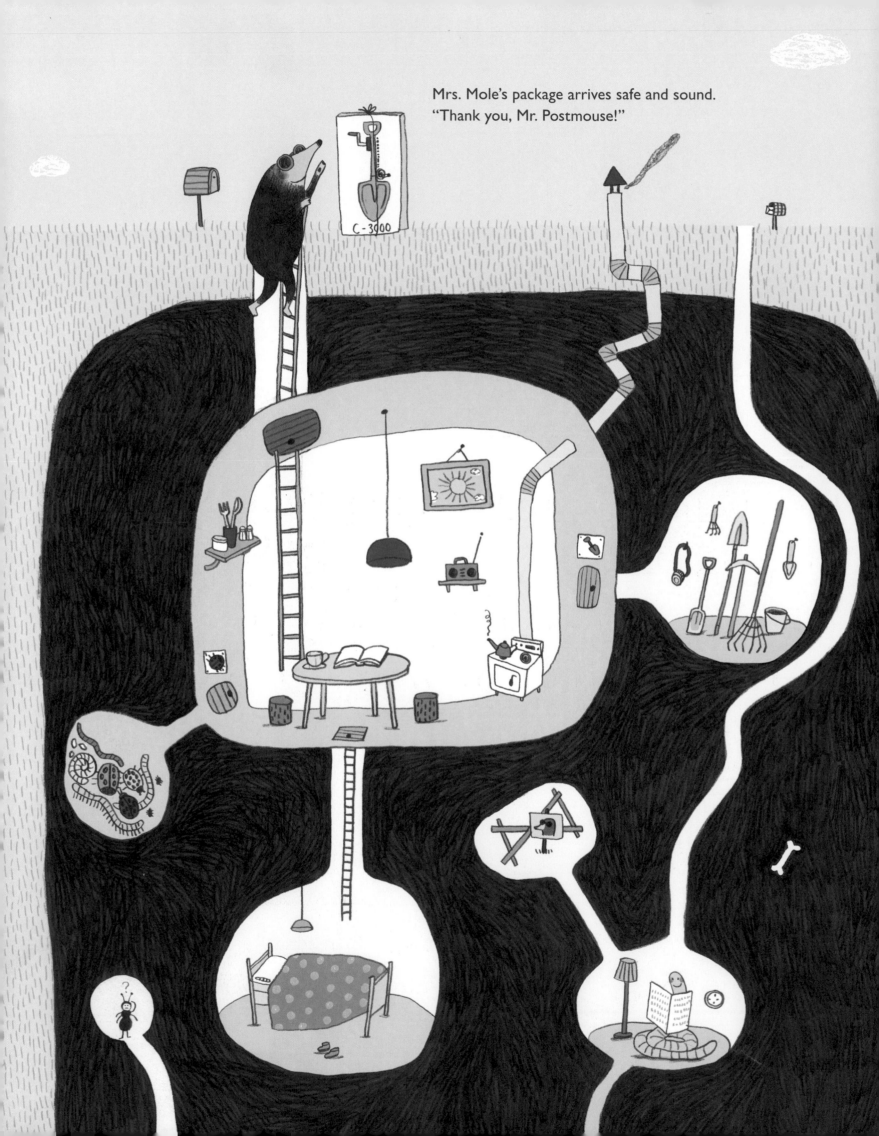

Mrs. Mole's package arrives safe and sound.
"Thank you, Mr. Postmouse!"

And it's a sweet treat for the Ants.

Down the lane, Mrs. Turtle unwraps two pairs
of zippy roller skates for her mobile home.

The Crocs' house is just next door.
(It's so very humid!)

Mr. Postmouse lets nothing stand in the way of his deliveries.

"Gurgle, gurgle!"*

*"Hello, Mrs. Octopus!"

Oh, look — it's a game of
hide-and-seek in the coral!

Ahh ... On dry land at last.
A little note for Mrs. Fly ...

And next it's Mr. Wolf's turn.

Shhh! Mr. Postmouse tiptoes quietly around the Bat Sisters' house.

At the Penguins' place, it's winter all year long. *Brrrrr!*

Mr. Yeti receives delicious tarts
from his cousin Yolanda. *Bon appétit!*

Then Mr. Postmouse heads back down to the valley. Whee!

"See you next time, Mountain Goats!"

Just a few more deliveries
to make.

This one is a
bit smelly ...

And this one is a bit worrying.

Now there is only one parcel left.
Who is it for?

Surprise! It's for Mr. Postmouse's son, Milo.
"Happy Birthday, my little mouse!"